For Lilu and Bodhi, who taught me
to love the early morning
—E.L.

For A & S
—P.Z.

Published by Two Lions, New York
www.apub.com

Amazon, the Amazon logo, and Two Lions are trademarks
of Amazon.com, Inc., or its affiliates.

ISBN-13: 9781542028837
ISBN-10: 1542028833

The illustrations were rendered in watercolor, pencil, and gouache.
Book design by Abby Dening

Printed in China
First Edition
1 3 5 7 9 10 8 6 4 2

Before the World Wakes

by **Estelle Laure**   Illustrated by **Paola Zakimi**

two lions

The nicest time of day is not when it's bright.

It is not when there is so much noise

or when we go from here to there
and there to here

and back again.

It is not bath time

or dinnertime

or even when we're playing
before we go to sleep.

My favorite time is when we slide out of bed
and everything is still gentle and quietish
and full of other people's dreams and sleeping.

We wrap ourselves in blankets,

and our toes squish into wet grass
that is cold but not too cold.

The stars say good morning at the same time
they say good night,
and we watch the moon pull them home,
as night and day hold hands.

Then the sky goes the color of a wish.
It's just for us.

The snails do a slow dance,
flowers turn their faces to watch,

and the crows and the sparrows and the magpies
start up their hollering and singing,
while the cedars and spruces and aspen trees
all whisper out their own song.

We join in because it's so good to say hello,
especially to a new day.

When we go inside, Mama asks,
"What do you do out there while the world is still asleep?"

"Nothing," we say, because sometimes it's special
to have secrets about trees that whisper
and snails who dance just for us.

But even more than that,
the real answer that we won't tell anyone,
not even each other,
is that the best part of being up
before the world wakes
is being together.

That is not nothing. It's everything.